# The Adventure Begins

Written by:
# Sammie Owens

Illustrated by:
# Artis Owens III

**MOLLY THE TURTLE**
The Adventure Begins

iUniverse books may be ordered through booksellers or by contacting:

iUniverse
1663 Liberty Drive
Bloomington, IN 47403
www.iuniverse.com
1-800-Authors (1-800-288-4677)

ISBN: 978-1-5320-7258-1 (sc)
ISBN: 978-1-5320-7259-8 (e)

Library of Congress Control Number: 2019904240

Print information available on the last page.

iUniverse rev. date: 04/12/2019

# The Adventure Begins

In a cool green pond, resting on a brown log, there was a turtle. She was a happy little turtle covered with green moss on her back.

Up pops a little grey minnow, "wake up Ms. Molly, how you doing today? I was wondering could you tell me one of your adventures?"

Molly had been on many great adventures. She loved to tell the pond family and friends about the things she had done and the places she had been. Molly had always wondered what was out pass the green scum of the pond. "Sure Skyp", said Molly "which one would you like to hear"?

"Why did you leave the pond in the first place asked Skyp?" The pond water was cool, lots of logs for sunning; plenty of good eating, many good friends, and it were a safe place. "I wanted to know what was on the other side of the ditch", responded Molly, so I ventured out.

One warm sunny day, I was slowly crossing the street in Masonville when ZOOM, a big red truck almost hit me.

I tucked inside my shell afraid to move. When I started to move again the truck stopped and headed back to me.

I tried to run but then a hand gently scooped me up and it all went dark.

The next thing I saw was a beautiful lady who takes me out and places me in a water container. I try to escape with no luck.

I was placed in the window sill of a box on wheels. I heard them call it an RV. I see lots of trees, ponds, and bridges pass by.

When the box on wheels stopped rocking, I'm then placed in a new rock pond beside two glass boxes inside a room.

This room was amazing! The walls were colorful, there were shapes and markings and music playing.

I look to one side and I saw two fish that were gold. I didn't know fish came in that color, all I had ever seen before were grey fish back at the pond.

I looked to the other side and saw shells with legs. I didn't know shells had legs.

I spoke to the shells and out pops two eyes on sticks. "Hey, what's your name" asked Molly. "I'm Joe," I live here with six other crabs". "Six" said Molly, "I can only see shells."

"We're hermit crabs, "said Joe, "we kinda keep to ourselves". "How long have you lived here", asked Molly? We don't rightly know answered another crab in a blue shell. Children watch and play with us. "We're called school pets", answered Joe. "I don't want to be a school pet," said Molly. But little did I know that was only the beginning.

"Weren't you afraid", asked Skyp. "There's no need to fear others because they look different. We're all the same underneath. Go on, the fireflies are stirrin', best be headin' home, that's a story for another day.

The real Molly the turtle that inspired this series.

The real Molly the turtle that inspired this series.

Printed in the United States
By Bookmasters